THE MYSTIC LEAGUE AND MEDUSA

MEGHANA MEDA

Copyright © Meghana Meda
All Rights Reserved.

This book has been published with all efforts taken to make the material error-free after the consent of the author. However, the author and the publisher do not assume and hereby disclaim any liability to any party for any loss, damage, or disruption caused by errors or omissions, whether such errors or omissions result from negligence, accident, or any other cause.

While every effort has been made to avoid any mistake or omission, this publication is being sold on the condition and understanding that neither the author nor the publishers or printers would be liable in any manner to any person by reason of any mistake or omission in this publication or for any action taken or omitted to be taken or advice rendered or accepted on the basis of this work. For any defect in printing or binding the publishers will be liable only to replace the defective copy by another copy of this work then available.

The Mystic League and Medusa is my First Book and I want to dedicate this to my Mother who has selflessly sacrificed her job career to nurture me since my birth. I am grateful to my Father and Mother who are my best friends. Without their love, caring, passion, continuous guidance and mentoring, my learning and writing journey wouldn't have been made so far.

Love You **Amma** (means *Mother*) & **Nanna** (means *Father*)!

Contents

Preface

My imagination of going on an Adventure inspired me to write this book. What the characters do on this journey is what I wanted to do on my own adventure. I hope the book will give a similar magical experience for the readers with the characters playing their roles in the imaginary world.

I would like to thank my parents who motivated and helped me in writing this book. They made me go further and stretch myself to complete this story and publish it. This is my first book which starts a new chapter of a writer in me at the age of 12.

Thank You!

Acknowledgements

It's a great experience in writing and publishing my first book to the world at the age of 12. I have learnt a lot in writing this book which will be the stepping stones of my writing journey ahead.

Thanks to my family & friends who encouraged me in this writing.

Thank You for reading this Book!

Foreword

"Education is to inculcate wisdom and share knowledge and to lead a fruitful and purposeful life"
- Renuka (My Grand Mother)

CHAPTER ONE

The Escape

It was late in the night when Sir George heard a loud noise coming from a cell in the prison. He strolled through the prison checking every cell on his way, but the prisoners were all asleep. He realized the sound was coming from the deepest cell in the prison. To get to the cell, a person had to descend a series of stairs, deep underground. Sir George grabbed his spear tighter by each step he descended. The closer he got to the cell; the louder footsteps became. Sir George stopped a few steps away from the prison cell, only to find a figure of a woman wearing a black robe.

The woman was facing the cell, and didn't show her face.

"How did you get out of your cell? Go back inside, or else," Sir George muttered.

"Or else what? There is nothing you can do to stop me!" The woman cackled.

"Else I'll call all the guards!" Sir George said with all the courage he could muster. But most of his courage had fled after talking with the woman.

"But I don't think you would have that chance." The woman said with a chuckle.

She turned her face to Sir George, and for the first time he saw her face. The woman's eyes were covered with her hood, but her face was wearing a sly grin. As the woman pointed her finger at Sir George, a blast of light erupted from it and shot him. Sir George collapsed to the ground.

The woman escaped from there, seen by no one. The head guard of the prison immediately sent a message to King Victor about the escape. King Victor and Queen Gloria were worried for the safety of their kingdom, as the woman who escaped was no ordinary woman. The King and Queen sent word to the Mystic League, hoping it would reach them wherever they were.

> "*Dear Mystic League*
>
> *You have to return back to Centaurus Peak immediately. Danger has fallen upon our kingdom. It isn't safe for you to be out there. A prisoner has escaped from the dungeons. This prisoner is very dangerous, more than you can imagine. Please return home safe and make sure to warn the leaders about this.*
>
> *King Victor and Queen Gloria*"

CHAPTER TWO

Fairy Forest

The four friends were on a trip to explore the Fairy Forest. The Fairy Forest was the most beautiful forest known. It was owned by the Fairies who made it. The four girls mounted on Speculo and he soared in the sky to land in the Fairy Forest. As Speculo landed in the center of the area, the girls looked around in awe. It was a breathtaking sight. The forest was filled with many different plants, some of which were enchanted by the fairies. The fairies had made their homes inside the various plants. The girls got off Speculo and told him to stay there.

The girls started roaming around the place, smelling the colorful flowers. The place was glistening with the fairy's magic. The girl's hearts were flying. Aura started running around in the magical dust and ended up tripping on a toadstool. That was when she realized it was the home of a fairy. The fairy living in the toadstool came out of her home upset. She had been napping and the loud 'thud' caused by Aura had woken her up. "Who are you people? I was having a lovely nap, and you woke me up! Had you fallen a little further you would have smashed that home over there!" The fairy screamed. The girls were surprised by the fairy's annoyance but still apologized. But by the time they did so, the fairy's ruckus had brought the attention of all the fairies nearby. The girls had never seen so many fairies at once. All the fairies had an annoyed look on their faces. They all seemed to be busy with something and then got disturbed by the screaming. The fairies took the girls to a tree nearby. The tree was the heart of the forest. It was a majestic tree which looked very old. It had many branches and its trunk was wide. The tree had a door at the bottom, so the girls assumed it was another home. The odd thing was that when the girls went near the tree, they got a sense that it was asleep.

The fairies called out to the tree. As they did so, the door opened and a fairy came out. The fairy was wearing a long dress made of beautiful flower petals. She was wearing a garland of tiny rose buds. Her wings had patterns that looked like flowers on them. Her name was Rose and she was the leader of the fairies. "What happened everyone? Why are you all here? Is there any problem?" she asked the fairies. "Yes, there is! These people came to our forest and disturbed our neighborhood. They almost smashed a home!" The fairies told her. The girls then interrupted and tried to defend themselves. "We didn't want to do so! Aura just tripped near your home by mistake and fell down!" The girls exclaimed. "Very well. You can explore our forest as long as you are careful not to trip over or smash any homes." Rose told them. "Thank you Rose." Hayley said and led the girls out of the area of homes. They entered a free space in the forest filled with plants and decided that it was the perfect place for them to have their lunch. They laid their mat on the grass and set up their food. The place was peaceful, and the only thing they could hear was the chirping of birds. The girls ate their lunch and talked for some time. Afterwards, they started to play and explore the plants. They experienced the magic of the plants too, as they were all enchanted. The girls had lodes of fun. They wanted to stay for longer, but they knew that they had to go. They wanted to make a stop near Coraline Bay to spend some time near the water and then go home. So, the girls made their way to Elorie's beloved dragon Speculo. Elorie mounted Speculo first and flew him to the entrance of the forest. Faith led Hayley and Aura there, and the girls mounted Speculo. The dragon shot into the sky again and headed for Coraline Bay.

CHAPTER THREE

A Worrying Message

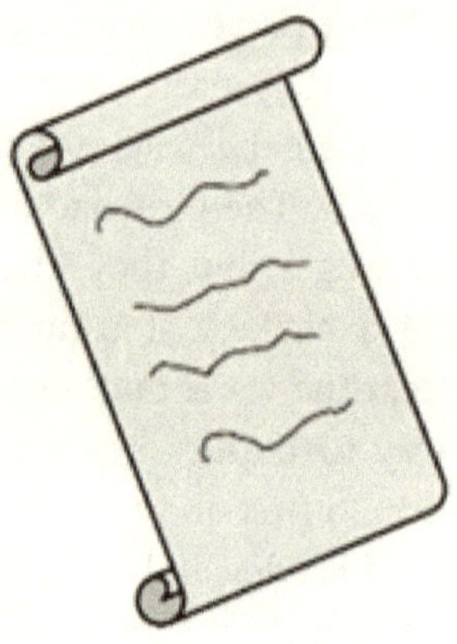

Speculo zoomed into the clouds to make the ride more fun for the girls. The girls were having so much fun they didn't realize how high up they were! Speculo dropped back down and landed on the shore of Coraline Bay. Aura quickly jumped of Speculo and dove into the bay. The girls slowly got of and left their things with Speculo. They ran to the water and sat on the sand, dipping their legs in the bay. Suddenly a glow came from the bay. The girls waited. Aura popped out of the bay and the glow stopped. Aura started swimming with her tail. She was the daughter of Aalto, the leader of the bay. Aura was a mermaid who had the power to transform into a human. She started singing a tune and soft waves started flowing towards the girls. The waves created a soothing music while the sun setted. The place was pleasant. As the cool breeze blew in the girls faces, they felt that nothing could go wrong at that moment. It was just then that a messenger of the kingdom started running towards the girls. He was calling out for Haley. Hayley stood up and waved towards the messenger. The messenger reached the girls and handed Hayley a scroll. "Princess Hayley, havoc has arised in the kingdom! The King is very worried. He said this message is very important! Please read it now!" The messenger explained. As Hayley read the message, her eyes widened and she was shocked. "We have to make a stop near every part of the kingdom. We have to warn all the leaders about this!" Hayley exclaimed. "We'll spread out then. I'll enchant everyone to the different parts of the kingdom. Aura can warn her father. Tell us what to say." Elorie told everyone. Hayley whispered what to tell to everyone and Elorie enchanted everyone to their parts of Centaurus. Once Elorie had warned Rose and the fairies, she got onto Speculo to pick up the girls. The girls flew back to Centaurus peak where the castle was. As they reached there, the King and Queen took them inside and locked the palace doors. "Mystic League, you have to be alert at this time. The prisoner who has escaped is not a normal person, and you should know that. Come inside and we are to have a meeting after dinner." Queen Gloria explained to the girls. The girls went inside to their rooms in the palace. The girls were known as the Mystic League as they would go around solving problems of the kingdom. The Mystic League was from different parts of the kingdom. They all would stay in the palace though, as they were important members of the Centaurus Council. The girls went to freshen up before they went down for dinner. Dinner was very quiet, as everyone was shocked by the news. They knew that they had to do something about the prisoner, but what could they do? Just when the girls thought that their simple adventure was over, they found out that their greatest adventure till now was yet to begin.

CHAPTER FOUR

The First Step

Once dinner was over, the King, Queen and the girls headed upstairs to the library for their meeting. The meeting had started. "As all of you know, the escapee has powers stronger than anyone can handle. Now that she is out she is very harmful. We have to catch her, but in a smart way. The last thing we want is for her to know that we want to stop her.

"If want to stop her we first need to know where she is." Faith replied. "I can figure out where she is. Let's go to the table over there." Said Elorie. Elorie took her bag and sat near the table where everyone gathered. She took out a crystal ball which was as clear as water. She placed the ball on the table, and lowered the hood of her cloak. Everyone was confused. How would they find the escapee with a ball? Elorie closed her eyes and started to murmur. It seemed like she was chanting something. Suddenly, the ball started glowing blue and violet shades. Everyone stared at it surprised. The ball started floating and that was when they realized that Elorie's black hair was floating too. The ball kept glowing brighter by the minute. Finally, the ball went down along with Elorie's hair. Elorie opened her eyes. Everyone was staring at her.

"She is in the Hidden Tower. I know how to get there. If we start tomorrow morning, and go on Speculo, we can reach there by afternoon. Its located in the South forests." Elorie explained. Everyone was surprised, but agreed with her. Hayley brought out a map and marked the place where they had to go to as well as Centaurus Peak. She gave the map to Elorie who put it in her bag. "What will we do when we get there though?" Aura asked. "We can place this mirror inside the tower. We'll be able to watch the tower from my other mirror then." Elorie replied. "Great, then it's settled. Tomorrow morning you girls can start to travel. We shall plan more after this step." Queen Gloria exclaimed. The meeting ended and everyone headed to their rooms.

Everyone was anxious about the journey the next day. As night fell upon the kingdom, they all slept.

CHAPTER FIVE

To Place A Mirror

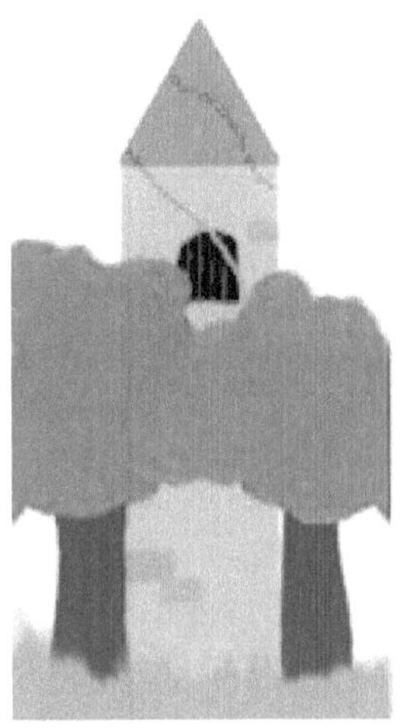

It had just dawned when the Mystic League had gathered with the King and Queen at the entrance of the palace, with all their things for the journey. "Are you ready?" Hayley asked the girls. "I think this is as ready as we can be." Aura replied. "Ok then, its time." Elorie said as she mounted Speculo, and directed him towards the edge of the peak. The girls bid farewell to King Victor and Queen

Gloria and left for the first step of their adventure.

On the way to the tower, the girls started discussing how they would get in the tower, and that too without getting the escapee's attention. That was when they remembered that the tower was built to keep the prisoner inside, but when the prisoner found a way to get out of the tower, they abandoned it. "Girls! We know that the tower has a hidden passageway inside it right! So, if we find the right part of the tower's base, we'll be able to get in!" Elorie exclaimed. "Right, then I can send the mirror to a corner with water!" Aura told the girls. The girls were happy with their plan, and continued to discuss it the rest of the way to the tower. Once they reached the tower, the girls told Speculo to wait there while they searched for the passageway. The tower was in the far corner of the South forests. It was an old tower and was covered in vines. It had moss growing between the stone bricks. The tower was surrounded by trees. The only way to enter the area was to go into a cave which was actually the entrance of the area. The place was well hidden, thus the name Hidden Tower.

The girls searched the base of the tower for any kind of symbol. Finally, Faith called out to the girls. The girls ran towards Faith, to find her staring at a cross mark engraved on a stone. Faith pushed the stone, and the girls stepped back. The wall of stone moved aside to give way to a dark passage. Elorie tapped her septor to the ground, and its blue gem lit up. The girls followed the path. They ascended a long line of stairs to finally reach a small room with a window. The window had a view of the whole forest. Hayley looked around to make sure that no one was there before climbing the last few stairs. The girls realized that the escapee wasn't there at that moment. Aura slowly formed a bubble of water with the mirror inside it. The bubble slowly drifted towards the corner of the room and popped behind some rocks. The mirror fell behind the rocks and was hidden from sight. The girls immediately descended the stairs and ran out the passageway. For all they knew was that the escapee was in the tower waiting for them. They hurried towards Speculo and mounted his back. Elorie tugged Speculo's reins and he flew out of the forest as fast as he could. But this time it wasn't because of excitement. It was because of fear.

CHAPTER SIX

A Strange Meeting

King Victor and Queen Gloria anxiously waited for the girls. They were worried about them. The monarchs waited in the library for any news. Finally, the girls had returned. The king and queen hurried to the entrance of the palace and welcomed the girls in. "So, did you place the mirror? Did anyone see you? Did you see the escapee?" King Victor kept asking the girls questions.

But the girls needed a break.

The girls went to their respective rooms to freshen up. As Elorie placed all her things on her table, she saw a figure of a person she knew she recognized, in the mirror. As she went closer to the mirror she could see more and more of a room. She placed her hand on the mirror and a blast of light threw her onto the floor.

"Just as I expected. Hello mother." Elorie said, staring at the mirror in anger.

"You've guessed it right. Hi Elorie." replied the figure in the mirror.

"What do you want mother?"

"I want you to join hands with me."

"That will never happen."

"If you join hands with me, we can conquer Centaurus together. Think about it, this vast kingdom in our hands!"

"If the kingdom goes into your hands there will be nothing but destruction. I won't let that happen."

"Even if you don't join me, I will complete what my father once started. Don't stand in my way. It will be dangerous for you. Think about it." The conversation ended.

The figure in the mirror had disappeared. Elorie put her cloak on and took her scepter, and headed to the library. By the time Elorie had arrived everyone was there, and were discussing what to do next. "Why are you so late?" Aura asked Elorie. "Um, I thought the meeting was in the throne room. I was waiting there." Elorie replied. "Fine. Anyway, we were discussing and we thought that it would be good if we first observed what she is doing. If you can place the mirror in this room, and enlarge it would be great." Aura explained to Elorie. So, Elorie took her mirror out of her pocket, and placed it in a nook on the second floor of the library. She then enlarged the mirror. They all gathered near the mirror to see if the escapee was doing anything at the moment.

Suddenly, a figure of a woman running into the room appeared in the mirror. The woman was wearing a black cloak. The hood of the cloak was covering her eyes. She had a scepter with an emerald gem on it. The woman had pale skin and black nails. The woman took a pot from the corner of the room and placed it in front of her. She snapped her fingers and a fire started to blaze below the pot. She pointed her finger at the pot, and water started to fill it. She then brought some jars from the shelf behind her. In one jar, there was a green stem which was as thin as a hair strand. She took the stem and put it in the water. She then poured one drop of liquid which looked like water in the mixture. After that, she put a crystal in the liquid. The ingredients went on for some time.

Finally, she took one bud of a flower and dropped it in the mixture. She stirred the mixture until it started to boil. She took a ladle of the liquid, which was now a glowing blue, and poured it in a flask. She made sure that the bud was in the flask too. She placed the flask on the other shelf where there were other flasks. A sly grin appeared on the woman's face. She snapped her fingers once more and the pot disappeared. She headed upstairs to a different room, leaving everyone confused.

Everyone was worried. What was she up to? Why was she grinning? What was that potion going to do?

Elorie then said, "She made an ash potion. Those are the ingredients for it. Whatever the potion drips on turns to ash. She is planning something with that. The Ignis flower bud is the thing she needs the most for that potion. We first have to collect all of those buds, and make sure she doesn't get any more."

Since Elorie was an enchantress, everyone knew she was the best with magic and potions. So, they all agreed with her. The Ignis buds they were searching for were extremely rare, and found in only one place in all the seven kingdoms. That one place was the Oswald Forest. The Oswald Forest was located in the kingdom of Orion. This kingdom was abandoned a long time ago. Legend has it that an Enchanter who could control the water waged a flood on the kingdom after they disagreed to surrender to him. The kingdom is covered by the Oswald Forest now. The center of the forest is a volcano. These rare buds are located at the base of the volcano.

"It will take two days to reach Orion. We better start tomorrow morning on our ship. Once we get there, we have to reach the volcano and gather all the buds." Elorie told everyone. "Then that is our next step." Hayley told everyone. The meeting then ended and everyone left.

Set Sail Ahoy!

In the morning, the girls got ready for their journey. Elorie gave the King and Queen a mirror which allowed them to communicate with the girls if needed. They needed all the equipment possible. The girls packed food, clothes and the equipment and stored it on Speculo. Unknown to everyone, Elorie kept a small pocket mirror with her. They flew to the shore where their ship was. They shifted all their things to the ship. It was time to leave.

The trip was going to be long this time. But the girls felt ready. They boarded the ship and set sail. As far as the girls knew, this trip was to obtain the buds. But to Elorie, it was to find out what her grandfather had started, and what her mother would do. The thought made Elorie nervous, but she had to keep it a secret. The girls decided that it was only fair that everyone took turns in steering the ship. Hayley was steering the ship, while Faith made sure that they had everything on the ship. Elorie enchanted some wind to get them started, and Aura pushed the ship further with waves of water. Everything was going well so far.

Once all the work was done, the girls decided to take a break. They talked about how they were going to get to the volcano, then they ate some food, after that, they played some games. The girls were starting to have some fun. Finally, some rocks came along and it was time for Hayley to go back to steering. It had become night by the time they could see an island. According to Faith's map it was the Ursa Island. Hayley steered the ship towards the island. The girls wanted to camp on the island for the night. They all took their mattresses and lanterns, and headed to find a nice spot to camp.

The island was mostly deserted. According to the legend even this island was a victim of the Enchanter. The starry sky was something the girls couldn't see at the palace. It was a mesmerizing sight. The girls fell asleep counting the many stars in the night's darkness. The next morning, the girls got onto the ship again and set sail for Orion. The sun was very bright and cheery. The wind blew in Faith's face as she steered the ship. Aura was swimming next to the ship. Everything was going well. All the girls were enjoying the morning.

Elorie though was planning something. Something the girls didn't know about. She was planning on how to change track from her friends. In Orion, there was a cave which held the history of all the families of Enchanters. Whichever enchanter stepped into the cave; their family's history would appear. Elorie had to go to that cave. After a long time of traveling, they had arrived near an island. That was the kingdom of Orion.

CHAPTER EIGHT

Off Track

The girls excitedly got off the ship. Since Elorie said that she would get their equipment, the girls were waiting at the shore. Meanwhile, Elorie went to the storage room of the ship, and took out a mirror piece she had been hiding in her pocket. She placed her finger on the mirror and the mirror started to glow. As the light faded, a figure appeared in the mirror. "Hi dear," The figure said.

"I've decided to join hands with you. No one knows about us yet. I'll be with the girls acting along. I'll report to you if they're up to something serious." "Perfect." The figure grinned.

Elorie placed the mirror back in her pocket and gathered the equipment. She hurried to the girls. They started their journey into the jungle. The girls made sure that they followed the map precisely, for the Oswald Forest was humongous, and very easy to get lost in. The girls headed south further and further. Finally, they stopped at a tree, tired, and decided to rest. Elorie told them that she would collect water in their flasks from the pond nearby. Elorie left to get the water, and left for a long time.

The girls took a long nap as they were tired from all the walking. When they woke up though, Elorie was still nowhere to be found. The girls searched all around, but couldn't find her.

Elorie on the other hand had found her way to the Enchanter's cave. What she didn't know was that she had gained a follower. When Elorie was near some big rocks in front of the cave, Aura had found her there, and had been following her since. Elorie chanted some words and the boulder blocking the cave moved aside. Elorie stepped inside the cave, but as soon as she did, she slipped down a slope. Aura without thinking, quickly ran after and leaped into the cave before the boulder closed. Both the girls slid down the slope to find themselves in a dark room. Suddenly, the torches in the room went aglow, and writing with pictures appeared on the cave walls.

Elorie and Aura were astounded. "Aura! What are you doing here?" Elorie asked shocked. "Making sure you're, ok?" Aura replied. "What are you doing here anyway?" "Don't tell the others. This may be shocking, but I want you to know that I am still who I am, no matter who my family is."

"My mother is Medusa. I am the escapee's daughter."
Aura was shell shocked.

"You are joking right?" Aura asked nervously. But Elorie shook her head in disagreement. "I have to know about my family. My mother wants to continue something that my grandfather had started. I don't know what that is, so I came here to find out." Elorie told Aura. Aura was shocked beyond imagination. "My mother thinks that I have joined hands with her now. If I didn't make her believe that, she would have harmed you guys by now." "Right now, all I can do, is follow you and stick to your plans. So, what are we doing now?" Aura replied. Elorie explained her plans to Aura, and the girls continued down the corridor to the section of Elorie's grandfather. When they read the writing, they were shocked. The Enchanter who had waged a flood on the six kingdoms was Elorie's grandfather. He had drowned all the kingdoms, except one. That was the seventh kingdom, Centaurus. Elorie's mother Medusa, wanted to complete her father's mission by burning Centaurus. Elorie was worried for the kingdom, and so was Aura.

"What do we do now? How can we stop her?"

"We're already collecting the buds, which means she can't make more of that potion. But I have to send her away. She can always escape from the dungeons. I have to send her into the mirror."

"How will you do that though?" "I have her trust, and I have a plan." The conversation ended, and the girls decided it was time to return to the others.

When they returned, the girls ran towards them waving happily. It had been a long day and the girls had to camp again. The next morning, the girls started their long walk again. Finally, they had reached the volcano. The girls were ecstatic. They ran around Searching for the buds. But they didn't need to. The volcano's base was covered in those buds. The girls took their equipment and started collecting the buds. Elorie told the King and Queen that they found the buds through the mirror. By the end of the evening, the girls had managed to collect all the buds. They followed their map towards their ship, and ended up reaching the next morning. This was going to be a happy trip back home. When the girls reached the palace, the king and queen were so relieved, they looked like they would jump. The second step to stop Medusa was done.

Joining Hands

Two days after the girls returned, Elorie told them that she had to fix her scepter, so she had to go out. They agreed so Elorie left. Elorie was actually headed to the Hidden Tower. She took her trusty dragon Speculo with her. Speculo was Elorie's first friend. So, he was used to Medusa. They flew to the hidden tower. When Elorie went inside, she saw her mother waiting for her.

"You came! I was starting to think that you wouldn't. So, what is the first step? What are we going to do? Maybe we can first collect the Ignis buds."

"No. First we should send the monarchs and the Mystic League away. Then panic will spread."

"You are right! But where do we send them?" "My power is in mirrors. If we put our powers together, we can send them all into a mirror."

"Perfect! You really are my daughter!" "Then the plan is settled.

You can send Flamma to get our victims here. We can cast the spell in the tower. Now I better go back. I'll come before Flamma gets them here." The conversation ended, and Elorie left.

Medusa was excited for the first step of her plan. When Elorie came back to the palace, she took Aura to her room, and explained the plan to her. She gave Aura a mirror and told her to keep it with her. Hopefully, their plan would go just as it should. Aura convinced everyone to go on a walk the next day. Elorie told them that she had to pick up her scepter from the mender, so she would join them on the way. To everyone, it was a normal walk and picnic. To Elorie and Aura, it was their chance to defeat Medusa. The girls were nervous. When everyone was sleeping, Elorie told Medusa to get the victims from Coraline Bay.

CHAPTER TEN

A "Normal" Picnic

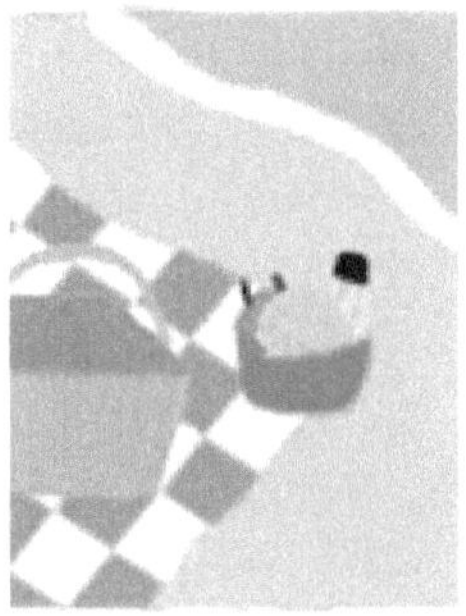

In the morning, everyone woke up, and got ready. They didn't have their breakfast as they were eating at the picnic. The food was all packed, and put in the carriage. They all got on the carriage, and their trip began. Everything was normal so far. They were talking about how nice a day off would be, and to get away from their duties. They all were having fun. Aura though, was very nervous about their plan. If their plan didn't work, then the monarchs and their friends would be in danger. They had finally reached Coraline Bay. Aura was practically sweating beads of sweat right now.

It was the time for Speculo's mother Flamma, to take all of them to Medusa. Elorie was already at the tower by then. Medusa and Elorie sent Flamma to get her friends. Everyone was having fun at the bay. Aura was sitting at the shore making sure she had the mirror. King Victor was eating lots of food, while Queen Gloria was collecting shells. No one was expecting danger at that moment.

All of a sudden, a large shadow crossed the sky. They all looked up, and saw a gigantic dark navy-blue figure in the sky. At first, they thought it was Evamore. But then they realized that it was too big to be him. Suddenly, the figure swooped down, and picked up all of them at once. They all were screaming. The figure was Flamma. Flamma took them to the hidden tower and dropped them in front of it. They all were confused. Why did it leave them here? That was when they realized that it must have been Medusa who had got them here. They all started trembling. Red mist started rising from the ground around them, and they were sent by the magic to inside the tower. That was when they saw Medusa for the first time.

Right beside Medusa though, they saw Elorie.

More than seeing Medusa for the first time, they were shocked to see Elorie beside her. "Elorie. What are you doing there! Get away from her immediately!" Hayley exclaimed. "Medusa is my mother, and I have joined her to demolish Centaurus." Elorie told them.

"Today I will be sending you inside a mirror such that you never return. You shall be trapped in it for eternity. After that we shall destroy Centaurus till every part of it is burnt to ash! Say goodbye to your precious kingdom!" Medusa cackled.

CHAPTER ELEVEN

Into The Mirror

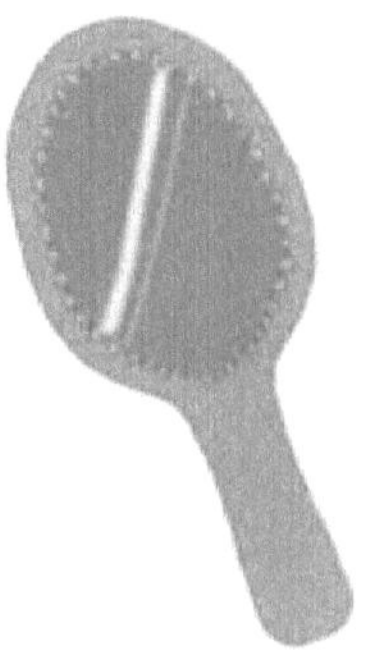

Medusa pointed her finger at them, and an evil smile grew onto her face. Elorie put her hands towards Medusa's finger to give the power. Aura held onto the mirror even tighter by the second. Each second became more intense. The room was so quiet, that they could hear their own heartbeats. King Victor, Queen Gloria, Hayley, and Faith were so worried, they looked like they were going to faint on the spot. Aura and Elorie were very worried too, but they held on to every last bit of hope left in them.

Finally, a blast of orange light erupted from Medusa's finger. A blast of violet shades with pieces of mirrors shot like a geyser from Elorie's hands, and connected with the orange blast. The blow of magic was heading towards them at the speed of light. It was just seconds before their lives would be trapped.

But just as the light was a millimetre away from them, Aura held out a mirror right in front of the beam. A big blast of light filled the room, and no one could see anything. Soon a white space filled the room, and only Elorie and Medusa were left in it.

Medusa knew what was happening.

"Elorie, you must forgive me, and most importantly forget about me. I was forbidden by the oath and revenge I swore to my father. You are far greater than any enchantress that I have seen, as your power comes from your heart. Use that power for good." Saying so, Medusa drifted away, and the white space around Elorie disappeared, leaving her in the room with her friends.

At last, when they could finally see, the only thing everyone saw was a mirror in place of Medusa. Elorie ran to the mirror and looked inside it. Her mother could be seen. Elorie stared at the mirror longingly. Aura came to console her. They rode Speculo home. The trip was silent. Everyone was still astounded. When they reached the palace, Elorie and Aura explained everything to them. It took a few days, but everything was back to normal. The kingdom was safe. Elorie had the mirror placed in a chamber in the palace locked. The Kingdom of Centaurus once again defeated an enchanter. As for the Mystic League, they had become more loved by their people.

The End